The author is a 13-year-boy who lo‿   ‿ks. Ever since he was about six, he'd write whatever   ‿o his mind, whether it was football or cricket or even things that are not real. Even for some of his school projects his mum would help him make a nice book by folding some paper and stapling it together so that he could write in it. He'd draw his own front cover and write what he'd like using his imagination and even write blurbs once he'd learnt what they are! As he got older, not all of his ideas were good or he didn't finish writing them, but he'd learnt not to give up on something he loves doing and soon as time went on and his books got better and longer, he thought it was time to get serious and share his ideas with the public, and here I am now writing the biography to my own, fully published book!

I would like to dedicate this book to my mother and father for always being there whatever the reason was, and sacrificing so much in their life for me and my siblings, none, absolutely none of this would be possible without them. Love you guys xxx

Shawn Vithanage

THE TALE OF ANNE CARTER

AUSTIN MACAULEY PUBLISHERS™

LONDON • CAMBRIDGE • NEW YORK • SHARJAH

A CIP catalogue record for this title is available from the British Library.

ISBN 9781398456884 (Paperback)
ISBN 9781398456891 (ePub e-book)

www.austinmacauley.com

First Published 2022
Austin Macauley Publishers Ltd®
1 Canada Square
Canary Wharf
London
E14 5AA

I would like to acknowledge Austin Macauley Publishers for being so helpful and nice to me also being very patient with me and being great publishers and people throughout the whole process, thank you very much.

Amorbis

Amorbis is the name of a planet of the Romanicus Anulus solar system. It is a beautiful place where love is spread throughout the one country that has formed there. Joy is always about. No problems have ever threatened the people of Amorbis and peace is always there. Over the years, since the start of humanity, Amorbis has become a heaven, lush green fields, towering buildings and gorgeous homes for everyone to live in and enjoy life. The only thing that inevitably happens to everyone is death. All boys and girls go to school and get ready for life, which enables them to become the future men and women of Amorbis, helping the planet thrive even more.

It seems as if every life is the same and ends up doing the same thing in this world, however, every life is unique, people go through different situations. They grow up to be different people with different personalities, different jobs and different lives. But the thing that all lives have in common is the fact that they enjoy every bit of it. Achievements such as becoming a professional athlete or good results in education are the little things which are enjoyed by family and friends.

Now, it sounds like the lives of the people in Amorbis are perfect and that the people don't have to do anything to earn this kind of life. But throughout their lives they work hard and the culture of Amorbis helps them reach a good level where they can support the people of their planet. All boys and girls grow up becoming men and women and once they reach that milestone, the one that they love the most, they will find. In this fantasy world, there is a beautiful forest, named as the 'Enchanted Forest', where all men propose to the love of their lives. It is a special place for a special moment…until the tragedy of Anne Carter. This tragic turn of events in her life changed the history of Amorbis.

FOREVER!

Anne Carter

Anne Carter was a well-known and much-loved woman in her town. She was a well-educated person and was a maths teacher in the local secondary school, Explenita Secondary School. She taught maths, which was her favourite subject. She had been a teacher at the school for three years, teaching mainly year 7s and 8s, but she had had a few A level students in her time at the school.

Anne was born in one of the wealthiest families in the region as her father owned a car company named 'Carter automobiles'. Her father was an incredible engineer and was enthusiastic ever since he learnt what cars were. He had progressed so far and was the first engineer to make an electric car to exceed 200 mph. Anne's mother was also a schoolteacher and Anne learnt a lot from her mother. She was actually her teacher in primary school. This inspired little Anne to become a teacher and also spread her knowledge just like her mother. She was well raised and was given responsibilities in the house from a young age, but the biggest responsibility was when her baby brother came when she was five years old. As time went by, her dream was becoming a reality. She started teaching her little brother once she started school.

Unfortunately, when Anne was 15 she noticed that her parents started arguing late at nights when she couldn't sleep. She knew her father went to the pub and came home drunk. Her mother would always try to confront her husband, but he was in a drunken state and wouldn't listen and would sometimes shout and be violent. Anne had always been taught and raised amongst peace and peaceful people. She had never witnessed anything like this. She would worry all night about what this unbelievable behaviour from her dad might lead too. She may not have been very young but she didn't understand. The more she heard, the more she thought, the more it worsened.

One typical night, Anne was, once again, wide awake at midnight listening to the shouts and cries which were coming from downstairs from her mum and dad arguing about things she couldn't understand. Suddenly, she heard what must have been a bottle of glass smash and scatter across the floor. But then it all stopped, as if time had gone extinct and life would no longer continue, but no, she was awake so it couldn't be. Then she heard the door of her house slam shut. She ran as quick as her legs could go, out of her room, down the stairs and into the living room where she saw her father bleeding with broken glass all around him and his shirt soaked with beer. But what worried her most was that her mother was nowhere to be seen. She must have left; her mother just couldn't take it. First of all, Anne grabbed her phone and rang 999 for the ambulance to take her dad to the hospital. He was bleeding quite badly, and it was just her instinct to get help in this type of situation. She was always proud that she was able to think quickly in desperate situations, a brief smile appeared on her face. But almost instantly, a thought hit her hard in the heart and into her pride as she realised that she could've stopped all of this from happening if only she'd gotten help for her parents…

But she didn't, she was too scared, too unsure, she just didn't understand. Anger, sadness, hate and anxiety all boiled up to a point where she just burst into tears.

Within a couple of minutes, an ambulance arrived and took her dad, whilst two of the medics checked on her, and asked her questions. She mostly answered, 'I don't know', but when they asked her what had happened, and to answer in best detail, she did. She started by saying that these arguments had been going on for a few weeks every night; she'd hear her mother cry whilst her dad shouted. She carried on until she finished at the present moment. Her dad was taken into the hospital and treated for his wounds. As her mother had left, one of her relatives came to pick up her brother and her so that they wouldn't be alone for the night. Her brother was confused and upset that their mother had left them and Anne was just devasted, all alone. Her father wasn't who he used to be and her mother had left. She didn't sleep the whole night and at around 8 a.m. in the morning, the next day, four people came; two she could recognise, the other two, she couldn't. There were two policemen and two other people. Once their aunt let the people in, they introduced themselves. There was Officer Fred Jameson, Officer Sandil Someratne, James Langley and Maddison Waiter. James Langley was a councillor and Maddison Waiter was from the local orphanage.

Police in Amorbis barely made any arrests during their career. In fact, their job in Amorbis is mainly to help the city or town they're in and to control the flow of traffic. This is similar with orphanages. They don't normally take in children who have nowhere to go, due to their parents breaking up or due to the conditions they live in. It's usually because one or both parents die. But in Anne and her brother, Alex's case, it was, unfortunately, because of a rare occurrence.

The police explained that they had to be taken away from their father as he had changed significantly and couldn't cope with his addictions. Therefore, he wouldn't be a suitable carer for them from now on until and unless he battles hard and overcomes his addictions and becomes the great person that everyone once knew. They said that what he had done to their mother in the past few weeks was unacceptable in society, and that he was going to a rehabilitation centre. Then the councillor joined in the conversation and said that what Anne had said was sufficient evidence to take her father away from them. She was ashamed of herself. The councillor told her not to worry as it was the most grown-up thing to say to the medics, and now they would be safe and live at the orphanage. As for their dad's car company, it was bought by Lyntosar, founded by Martini Lyntosar, another good car brand. Then Maddison started explaining about the orphanage they were going to be at. There were 24 other kids and six other members of staff. Maddison promised that they wouldn't be separated and that they would be in the same room, with two beds in it. This made Anne feel better, so after breakfast they went with Maddison to the Orphanage. They were taken on a tour, which ended at their room.

The orphanage was amazing, and had a big garden with trees scattered around, a few of them were apple and pear trees. Most of the kids there were younger than her and quickly made friends with her brother, but not her. But there were a couple of teens who were kind and friendly, and gave a warm welcome to Anne. She didn't know any of them as they didn't go to her school, and she had never seen them around town either, probably because the staff go out and get stuff rather than them. Anne was really happy that this turned out well and everyone here was so nice, but the fact that her mother had left still upset her. She just couldn't let go. But she realised she had to move on from this and continue her life.

So as days turned into weeks and weeks turned into months, she worked hard to reach her dream and become a teacher. After a few years of determination and hard work, she finally became a teacher and applied to work at Explenita Secondary School.

As time went by, she met a handsome man named, Harry Falkner, with whom she started going out with. Harry was a builder who worked for Constructium Builds, a company that builds homes and even majestic buildings. Anne met him on a cold bitter evening when she was walking home from school when it started raining. She was only wearing a cardigan, not even a jacket, and didn't have an umbrella. That's when Harry pulled up in his Lyntosar S-200, a sports car. He offered her a ride back to drop her off at her house. Anne gratefully accepted the offer and hopped into the insulated car. They both chatted throughout their journey, talking about their jobs and their past. Harry felt sorry for Anne after hearing about her mother running away. However, just like Anne, he was quite mad at how her dad behaved. She said that her dad still hasn't learnt to control his addictions and issues. After about 20 minutes, they arrived at Anne's house. She thanked Harry and asked him if he wanted to come to her house on Saturday night for dinner. He immediately said yes, and then got in his car and headed home. After a few months together, their relationship got stronger and stronger.

But one sunny day, Anne asked if Harry would like to go on a picnic with her to the Enchanted Forest that afternoon, but he replied with a no. She didn't go onto question him, as there must have been a good reason and she had to show him that she trusted him. Instead, she asked if her brother wanted to go as she'd already made the food and couldn't let it go to waste, and she could tell that she wasn't going to be able to eat all of it on her own. Her brother said he'd love to have a relaxing picnic, especially since he'd been working really hard at his job. He said he'd be able to come at 4:00 p.m. As she'd got the food ready, she packed it all in the picnic basket and marked the homework that her pupils handed in for the next couple of hours. At about 3:30 p.m. she cycled to her brother's house where they both went to the forest in his car. Once they arrived, they entered the forest and found a nice spot surrounded by flowers and trees. Before they started eating, she got all the plastic packaging and went to find the nearest recycling bin to put them in. This was the first time she had been in these woods, so she didn't quite know where a bin was, but a couple of minutes later she found a bin, with a bench next to it. She was shocked and distraught at what she found over on the bench. It was Harry! He was sat there kissing another woman. Anne was frozen, not even a peep was able to squirm through her sealed lips. She was devastated. Harry said he wasn't going to be able to come to the picnic today, and she'd believed him. She put all her faith and trust in him, and he did this to her. Cheat on her! She was full of hatred, regret and sadness, the one person who would possibly have become a part of her family and would've made her happy, especially as she'd already lost her mother and her dad wasn't with her anymore, had cheated on her. She started running as fast as she could, her tears blowing off her face and falling to the ground. She couldn't contain her feelings and once she fell over, she went beside a tree and just sat down on top of some damp, cold moss. She sobbed for minutes but still couldn't control herself. The broken twig that was beside her was a metaphor to her heart. She was insecure, she'd lost too many important, close people in her life, and this had crossed the line. She couldn't take it. Questions raced through her mind, 'How could he do this to me?' or, 'Why me?' or, 'What have I done to deserve this?' Her empty heart, leaking love, and filling with hatred. Strong thoughts filled her mind, she hated Harry, she hated that girl, but she also hated her LIFE. There was nothing left for her in this world. She took out her small pocket knife and sharpened a long, thick stick to ultimate sharpness and…

KILLED HERSELF!

Changed History

Her brother still sat worried and got quite impatient about now. He wondered what his sister was doing, or where she was, maybe she was lost, or maybe the bin was far away. He waited a bit longer, as he couldn't just leave his sister all alone in the woods, especially as the sun was setting.

After waiting for about 15 minutes, he couldn't keep his patience in. He was simply too worried. He called the police and reported his sister missing. The police said they'd be able to help. Alex was hopeful that his sister would be out there, waiting for help. The police arrived at the entrance after five minutes, which is where Alex was waiting for them. They'd brought a helicopter with them as well as it had a wide-range light, which was needed if they were to find anyone tonight, as it was dark. Once everyone was ready, they got to work. Although cases like this were very rare, the police were still trained for this. Alex went along with the police, and whilst they were searching, he said she may be lost somewhere close to a bin as she went to find one to put their plastic in. They kept searching as time went on but were unsuccessful. After about half an hour, they found a trail of plastic which was scattered along the forest floor. This was a sign; however, it was a sign which worried all of them. They followed the plastic in hopes of finding Anne alive. They were only granted one of their conditions. They found Anne, but she wasn't alive. They were all in shock, and her brother was devastated. The police needed to investigate this unreal scene which had taken place.

Unfortunately, they had to take Alex into questioning as he was a suspect, who may have been the one who killed Anne. He didn't fight or argue with the police for this action, as he wanted to find justice for his sister. He knew justice never came to her in her life, well, now was his time to try; so, he went back with a couple of policemen as some others stayed behind to close the area and investigate who or what did this. It could even be classified as suicide, but they would need more evidence to prove this.

Once Alex arrived at the station with the policemen, he was taken to the interrogation room to be questioned. Once they got finished and heard what they wanted to, he was told to stay for the night, which he was okay with. But he did request a policeman to get his car for the next morning. Alex couldn't really sleep with all of this on his mind. He wondered how his sister had died. He didn't want to overlook it, but he wanted answers. All his life, he always had questions himself and questions asked to him, just like a few minutes ago, but he never got answers. He wanted justice! Eventually, he drifted off to sleep and woke up early in the morning. He was offered breakfast at the police station, but politely declined and went outside to find his car. He thanked the policemen and went back to his home. On the way, he stopped by the Enchanted Forest and saw it was closed off. He knew there was nothing left for him to do and that the police had it all under control; so, he carried on with his journey. On his way, he called his wife to say everything was okay and that he was hungry. She said she'd make breakfast by the time he came home.

At the site, they collected as much evidence as they could, such as the sharp stick, pocket-knife, even blood samples to see if she was poisoned rather than stabbed to death. After trials, it was clear that she wasn't poisoned, or drugged in that case. The police had already got all suspects' fingerprints and then checked the fingerprints on the pocket-knife and stick. The results were as shocking as the news of her death. After checking the results thoroughly, the police force could, unfortunately, conclude that she had killed herself. It was SUICIDE.

Everyone was shocked, the news spread around like wildfire. There weren't usually cases of suicides, and the irony was that it was now exactly 10 years since her mother had left. Rumours went around saying that their family was cursed and that her brother would now follow in his dad's footsteps.

To Alex's relief, once the news and rumours reached them, his wife didn't believe them and knew he wouldn't do anything like that. Alex thought himself lucky to have such a woman as Juliet as his wife. She always believed in him through tough situations and didn't ask for anything apart from spending time with him.

They both ran their bakery together. Their bakery was the only one in town, but it had such a good reputation that orders came from people in cities and towns outside of theirs.

After the discovery of Anne's death and how it happened, a funeral was planned and the date was set to the fifteenth of April. Many people attended her funeral, but what caught

Alex's eye was the mysterious figure of a woman always at the back. As he was Anne's brother, he was the one who led the funeral and didn't get the chance to investigate. By lunchtime, the funeral was over, and everyone started going home, but the mysterious figure had already left, and he couldn't seem to find her anywhere. Before he wanted to ask people about her, to see if they knew, he stopped to think what was making him do this. What was making him so interested to find out more about; as if it was someone he knew, someone he'd missed the whole of his life and was close to him like…like his mother! It couldn't be…could it? She was long gone and everyone knew it. It'd been ten years, why would she come now? It's not like she knew that Anne had died and wanted to see her body. He shook it off his mind before he got too involved into it and got himself into a mess. Especially as acting out of the ordinary would encourage the people of the village to believe the stupid rumour, which he wanted to end. So, he headed back home in a normal manner, greeting people along the way. However, he still got the feeling that this wasn't the end of it.

Detective Alex

"I just don't know who it was darling, it's just the feeling I got, I mean, why would a random woman turn up out of nowhere, wasting her Sunday morning at a funeral. I mean, out of all the things for a typical woman to be doing, she comes to a funeral," explained Harry.

"I know darling, but maybe she's not a typical woman, or maybe you're imagining women wrong. I mean, how do you know what's typical for a woman to do? you're not a woman," replied Juliet.

"You're right, sweetheart, I can't judge, maybe it's something she likes doing," admitted Harry. "Although, I must say it is rather weird popping to someone else's funeral." They both left it there and enjoyed movie night with their roast chicken, boiled vegetables and wine.

Down in the police station it was very different, most forces were out investigating the deaths, which were suddenly starting to increase. The pattern that the police seemed to find after investigating every death was that it always turned out to be suicide, but another factor made it weirder…

All the deaths were women.

News was spread verbally, through television and the newspapers. Harry was concerned.

"Honey, do you think this sudden uprise in suicides have anything to do with my sister's death?" asked Harry. This created a glum, intense atmosphere, as if something was haunting the place. Juliet broke the silence.

"Maybe honey, I do sense something wrong here, not only have there been suicides and not murders, they have all been women. But I only know as much as you do," said Juliet "maybe you should go and ask the police station for more information about this?" suggested Juliet.

"Good idea, darling, I'll go and do that; can you manage the bakery on your own, it shouldn't be difficult as it shouldn't be busy today," said Harry.

"Oh, you know I can, darling, just don't take too long, please, and don't get too fussed over all of this," explained Juliet.

"You have my word sweetie; I'll be back by lunch." He kissed her on the forehead and got his hat and took off. He parked in front of the station, and went straight in. He greeted the Officers who went by and went to the front desk. Officer Sandil Someratne was there.

"Mornin', Officer, are you off duty today?" asked Alex.

"Yes, I was up at the site yesterday, but they told me take phone calls today, I'm guessing you're here to ask about the increase of suicides among women?" said Officer Someratne.

"Why, yes, actually, I am here about that. Don't you find it strange that people are killing themselves, and it's happening a lot now,?" said Alex.

"Well, I'd find anyone killing themselves a bit strange, wouldn't you?" backfired the Officer.

"Yes, but haven't you noticed that it all started off after my sister committed a suicide. It's as if some sort of trend has started, but why would people just kill themselves for a trend?" questioned Alex.

"Maybe all women have a soft spot where they can't stand their boyfriends cheating on them, I mean, I would be very annoyed if my wife cheated on me," he explained.

This intrigued Alex; he wanted to know more now.

"Why would you say that? Officer Someratne?" asked Harry, wanting to know more.

"Well, yesterday my brother's girlfriend killed herself after she found out that he was cheating on her. Quite unfortunate," Officer Someratne said.

"Hmm, thanks for the info, Officer. I better get going now, have a good day," said Alex.

As he was going home, he stopped at the Enchanted Forest, and, as he thought, there were forensics and police everywhere on their side of the barriers. Alex knew there was no point of him staying and staring at the forces at work, so he decided to go. As he was walking to his car, an old man walked up to him, looking quite angry.

"Look what the men of your generation are doing to the women. Back in my day, women were always treated well, and a divorce was never recorded until this decade," he bellowed at Alex.

"I'm sorry, but if it makes you feel better, my wife and I are living happily together. In fact, my wife and I are the ones running the bakery on Vine Street," said Alex, proudly.

"Hmm, I see. Well, I'll have to drop by then and get something to eat." the old man said. They both chuckled.

"Of course, that'd be great. Have a good day." Alex said to the old man and left, to go home. A few minutes later, Alex arrived and was warmly welcomed by his wife with a mug of hot chocolate. It was quite bitter outside today, so he accepted it gratefully, and his wife asked him if he learnt anything knew.

"Officer Someratne was on duty today and was happy to speak about it. He did say something which was useful to me. He explained that his brother's girlfriend killed herself yesterday as he was caught cheating on her," summarised Alex.

"That's awful, but the suspicious thing is that didn't your sister have a boyfriend," remembered Juliet.

"Oh yeah, do you think that all of these are related to complications in relationships?" but suddenly changing the subject, "Thanks for the hot chocolate, honey, but I think I'm going to pay him a visit. It's quite ironic actually, as he was one of the people interviewed by the police. The police only interviewed people who were in the forest at the time, after checking the security cameras. Which means, although my sister said he couldn't come, he was able to, and most likely with someone else. I think I have his address from when she texted me to pick her up from there. He seemed like a nice guy, but now I know what type of person he might actually be. Right, I'm off." So, for the second time today he took off in his car.

After a few minutes, he arrived at the address and knocked on the door numbered 7, which was the one written on his text message from his sister. He opened the door and as expected, Harry was there.

"Ah, I remember you, you're Anne's brother, it's quite chilly today, do come in. I've heard a lot of good things about you." Harry shared with Alex. However, Alex wasn't amused with his small talk. Harry was acting as if Alex didn't know anything, but he played along with it to get him to speak later.

"Yes, me and my sister did get on well together, she also said nice things about you," he replied, trying to spot a reaction of guilt appear on his face.

"Would you like some coffee?" Harry asked.

"No, my wife made me hot chocolate before I left. If you don't mind, I'm going to ask you some questions about your relationship with my sister," Alex said. Harry looked surprised but answered calmly.

"All right, I don't mind," Harry said cautiously.

"Okay, firstly, what were you doing while my sister and I were at the picnic in the Enchanted Forest? The picnic you were supposed to be at!" asked Alex.

"Umm…well, I mean… I had some work to do, you know," Harry stuttered whilst speaking, which showed Alex that he wasn't telling the truth and Alex knew the truth anyway.

"No, I don't know," he said, trying to get Harry to say more.

"Yeah… umm… well it's busy these days, at the construction sites,"

"So, is that the TRUTH?" asked Alex immediately after the last answer.

"Yeah, what else do you expect from a guy who works hard," said Harry. *'Hard work', you can say that again,* thought Alex.

"Nice try, smart guy but, you see, I know you were at the Enchanted Forest at the same time as us, presumably with someone else. You were interviewed by the police, weren't you? They only interviewed people in the forest who were

26

already there when my sister and I entered and the people who cane in just after her death," explained Alex. Harry was blushing, he'd been outsmarted.

"Well, yes, I did get interviewed but what does that mean?"

"I suspect that you were cheating on my girlfriend, which made her kill herself!" bellowed Alex, with tears welling up in his eyes. The tension between them was tight now and it got to a point where Harry was threatening him.

"I suggest you leave my house before things get messy; don't you think!" roared Harry. Alex was never a coward, but he didn't want to cause a disturbance in the neighbourhood, so he left without saying anything. He needed to do one more thing to confirm he was correct, hopefully, it'll go according to his plan. He went to the police station in his car and when he went in, Officer Someratne was still at the reception desk.

"Hello again, Officer, still on duty, I presume?" Alex asked, whilst greeting Officer Someratne.

"Yeah, isn't it obvious,?" said Officer Someratne, stating what a silly question Alex had asked. However, Alex only wanted to start a conversation, but it didn't really work, as Alex had found out.

"What do you want? I haven't got all day, you know," he spoke. Alex didn't want to get the policeman angered so he cut to the chase.

"Okay, this is going to sound crazy and stupid, but I think I know who the cause of my sister's death was and why. I also need your help to check something for me. Can you check the security cameras for any people for me, on the day of my sister's death,?" said Alex.

"WHAT! That's incredible, let's find out if your theory is correct, but can I trust you?" Officer Someratne asked cautiously.

"Yes, of course, I want to solve this mystery as much as you do," Alex replied. With that said, the Officer went through the camera recordings, and they went through the people who walked into the forest that day. At 9 a.m. Mr Hobart, who works at the Local Fish'n'Chips shop, entered the forest with his grandson and left at about 10:30 am. After that, Mrs Miller went in as well, with a picnic basket, and her husband Mr Miller. This was not the evidence Alex needed, but he waited patiently. Eventually, after seeing a lot of people enter the Enchanted Forest throughout the day, he spotted a notorious figure. It was Harry, and as he had suspected, he was with another woman, holding hands whilst entering the forest. He was correct, no wonder his sister killed herself. But these were all thoughts, too much rage had accumulated inside of him, and he couldn't even speak, and be proud of himself for solving the case. Officer Someratne just gazed in amazement that Alex had done it! He'd solved it! But looking into Alex's eyes, he could see that he was raged, annoyed, and wanted revenge! He started talking to lower the tension that was built.

"So, what do you want to do now? Now that you know it was him who has done this, and who has started this treachery in Amorbis," asked Officer Someratne, quite loudly, just to get Alex's attention, and take him out of the state he was in.

"I want him arrested!" Alex roared, then all emotional, "I mean, how could he do this to my sister, there's only a divorce once or twice a year, but nothing like this leads on from it," he said, whilst wiping his tears away.

"Yes, we must arrest him, not because you said so, but because he deserves it. I'll send some Officers right away; do you want to come?" he spoke.

"Yes!" Alex said with content. Of course, he wanted to see the person who led his sister's suicidal thoughts go to jail.

Four police Officers and Alex arrived at about 2:47 p.m. at Harry's house and were armed. One Officer used a battering ram to break the door open, as Harry wasn't opening up. After that, they entered and shouted, "Anyone in the house!" but it was silent. Alex didn't want to give up there, so he told two Officers to go upstairs and search for him, whilst he and the other two looked downstairs. After searching for a few minutes, Harry was finally found and arrested.

"Enjoy your time there with no women, Harry!" Alex taunted. Harry snarled back at him.

"I'll get you back, oh don't you worry, I'll get you!" he said surprisingly calmly, but an angry calm was how to describe it.

"Well, I can see you'll be locked up for a long time," Officer Someratne said jocularly, and everybody laughed, even Alex, satisfied that Harry was where he belonged. He had done what he had to and at the end of the day, it was all well for him.

The Upbringing

People just kept disappearing. But not only did that confuse the police force but it was something that they could not stop, something that would not be stopped. Anyone who ventured into the Enchanted Forest would always come back pale as a sheet of paper. Every single person would come back and report their horror to the police. It was the same thing over and over again. Ghosts! 'Ghosts' was the one word which was listed on every report from the citizens who, unfortunately, went into the Enchanted Forest. Its reputation had plummeted down and even stopped tourists from staying in the town. Many locals had dubbed it the 'Haunted Forest' due to what was going on. That was the thing, no one knew what was going on. However, one suspicious bit of evidence was that everybody who witnessed a ghost said that it was a female. They said that she would just stand there looking straight at them, mentally torturing them. But the last bit of information that always appeared was that the figure looked like Anne Carter! When this news reached Alex, he was shocked. This meant that, somehow, his sister was now a ghost and spooking everyone who entered the Enchanted Forest. He couldn't understand why she'd do that to all the people in the town, but he could understand if she'd do it to Harry. This was confusing and he couldn't wrap his head around as to why his sister would do that. He'd known her his whole life and she never had those kinds of feelings towards a lot of people, especially innocent people she'd never even met. The question of how his sister had been turned into a ghost was beyond his thought process and knowledge, but the question of why was thinkable. How hurt was she, after she'd found out Harry was cheating on her? If she was doing this then she must be emotionally hurt, badly, Alex thought. But he understood that thought, as he'd also be pretty hurt if Juliet cheated on him. But the fact that she was taking it out on everyone must mean something else was wrong, why did she suddenly hate everyone now? He couldn't figure this out on his own and decided to go to the police headquarters. There, he thought, he'd get more information about these sudden ghost sightings people have been having. After finishing of his morning coffee, he left swiftly, eager to get some answers. As usual, after about four minutes he arrived at the building which were the police headquarters. As he entered, he saw that it wasn't Officer Someratne, but an Officer he'd never seen before. He hoped that he would be willing to share information about the ghost of his sister, just like Officer Someratne shared information with him.

"Good morning, Officer, how was your day so far?" Alex asked, trying get a good impression on the Officer, not just to get information out of him but because he always thought it was a good idea to always gain policemen and policewomen's trust to keep a good atmosphere around them. Amorbis may have been a world which contains love and joy, where happiness is all about, but when it comes to police Officers, they have to do their job the way it should be done. So, getting on the good side of the police is always good, which is why Alex did just that.

"Good, how about yours, young man," The policeman asked. Alex didn't find it weird that he referred to him as 'young man' as he did seem much older than him.

"Hmm…how do you say it…ah! My day was interesting," Alex said, being honest. The policeman chuckled; Alex got the impression that the policeman was quite nice.

"So, Officer, I haven't ever seen you around here, are you new here?" Alex asked with curiosity.

"Why yes, young man, I have just moved here. I used to work in the other city, next door, but I started working here since I moved, which was yesterday," The old, but surely experienced Officer said to Alex. Alex saw this as a good start to gaining the Officer's trust.

"So, Officer is it ok if I ask you some questions about the recent sightings of ghosts which have occurred in the Enchanted Forest, People say she looks like my sister," He asked and explained, although, not with great detail as it just occurred to him that the Officer didn't know his sister, but surely, he'd work it out. Alex was correct.

"Ah, your sister is Anne Carter, is she?" he asked rhetorically, "I'm sorry to hear about her passing, young man. So, if she is your sister that means you must be…" he paused as he didn't know Alex's name, so Alex finished it for him.

"Alex, sir, Alex Carter," He said proudly and he should be proud of himself for what he has done and how he has coped with the troubles in his life.

"Well, Alex, you're in luck because I'm willing to help, you seem like a wonderful lad," he said, "I don't think I know a lot more than you do as people haven't described her differently, mostly because they didn't seem to get a good look at her and see what she does. But I do now that she seems to say, 'revenge' and, 'Harry will pay' before she leaves them traumatised," he explained. This didn't surprise Alex, but he thought he should return a favour to the old Officer and explain what he knows.

"Sir, I think I know why she says that. The one which includes Harry is because she used to go out with a guy named Harry, but when her and I went for a picnic in the Enchanted Forest, he had said he couldn't come, but in the end, my sister found out he was cheating on her with another girl," Alex thoroughly explained.

"Oh, that is quite unfortunate, I've heard something like this is extremely rare, and hasn't happened in a while." The old policeman stated. Right after he said that another person with shock and worry painted on his face entered shouting to get the Officer's attention. Alex moved out of the way, but just enough so that he could hear the conversion which was about to commence.

"Officer, Officer…" the man said, stopping to take a breath after running in quickly to report what seems to be an urgent report, "I saw the ghost of Anne Carter, but this time there seemed to be more women spectres flitting around with her, but they were silent, oh, it was traumatising. Then she came up to me, about a metre away, and brought a knife out, and I ran all the way here, oh, it was terrifying!" he explained swiftly, bottling his emotions up to the brim. Then it exploded, he burst into tears, the experience had mentally destroyed him.

"Now, now, calm yourself down, it's okay, you're safe," the Officer said, reassuring the sobbing man.

"Looks like my sister continues to cause trouble…" he stopped, thinking whether he should say what he was thinking of doing, it was crazy! "But I need to find out what's going on, I may have a better chance than anyone of not reaching to that kind of point, I mean, she is my sister, I'm fairly sure she wouldn't do that kind of thing to me," He blurted to the Officer with no regret, he guessed that the Officer would try and stop him. But he himself knew that he was unsure.

"Are you out of your mind, young man, this is outrageous, you can't be sure you will be safe. I'm sorry to say this, but if the way you described your sister is true, and I do believe you, then there's no way that is who she previously was" Officer said stating the obvious facts, "Wouldn't it be better to just shut the Forest down and keep everyone safe."

"Are you kidding! Just because my sister wants revenge doesn't mean other happy couples shouldn't get to propose in that Forest, it also doesn't mean that everyone should be bound from it, and anyways they're ghosts, closing the forest won't do anything bad to them, they can just fly out of there" Alex countered. Alex was right, it was a place that everyone could enjoy, the historic Forest. He knew what had to be done. The Officer was now busy taking care of the traumatised man, so Alex abruptly left to do what he intended to do. He got in his car and headed to the Enchanted Forest. As he was driving, he thought of what could happen. He had to be honest with himself, he didn't know exactly what he was doing and had no plan. It seemed very stubborn of him, the only thing encouraging him to this was the will power of overcoming this anger and helping out the people of his town. He thought no more. He arrived. He knew what to do.

He got out, took a deep breath, snuck past the police's 'do not cross line'. He glimpsed back to what may be his last time seeing his town, and then ventured into the haunted forest, not knowing what to expect. It took him a while to get back to grips of the right paths not to get lost, but he could not understand what had become of the forest. Tree scratches were everywhere, plastic scattered amongst all the fallen leaves. But another less appealing feature he spotted after getting deep into the forest. Blood! Stained all over the floor and soaked into the tree. This was shocking, whatever was going on in here, Alex knew he must find out. But safety was always on his mind. What if the new Officer was right and his siter had completely changed. Well, he knew he couldn't go back now. But what he saw next, stopped him right in his tracks. It was his sister! But in ghost form. He made eye contact, and she looked back, surprised, she didn't look at all murderous. Maybe he was right, maybe because she was his sister, she wasn't trying to kill him. But he didn't want this tension to carry on, wondering if his sister's mind would suddenly change if nothing was done. So, he cautiously began speaking.

"Anne, is that really you?" he asked tentatively.

"Alex, you came, but why?" she replied, acting innocently, as if he didn't know about her torturous doings.

"Anne, there have been so many reports that you tried to kill people and that more female ghosts like you were torturing people!" he said, in a way not to anger her. He was taking in so much pressure, and still couldn't believe he was talking to his sister. However, his feelings were mixed, but for now, the sight of his sister drowned the negative feelings and he was staying clam. But unfortunately, he could see her mood change.

"Alex, be reasonable, you must know what happened to me. All those investigators, forensics and police looking into my case, surely they must have figured it out by now and told you!" she said in, a now neutral voice, but still keeping up the innocent talk.

"Yes, I know and I already got revenge for you. You need to stop this. Harry is in jail, and I'll make sure he is for a long time," he said trying to reassure her.

"Sorry, Alex, but I think it's time to end the suffering for everyone," then suddenly the other female ghosts came out, "see my followers here, they also have been cheated on by their boyfriends, we think it's enough. I'm sorry but you're too late."

"I know you're not doing this to help people, life is not just all about love, there are other things to do. Plus, not everyone will cheat. It's your resent towards them!" he said, not caring about what he knew she could possibly do to him. But surprisingly, she stayed calm, pale, just staring right at him. Adrenaline was flowing through him, like he'd never felt before. His heart rate was beeping so quickly that he couldn't keep up with what was going on. What was going to happen! What was his sister planning? He couldn't stay here, he had to go and warn the people of his town, to prepare, for whatever was going to happen. He turned to see his sister. But he was too late. She'd vanished. Time was of the essence and he had to hurry, no matter where his sister was and what she was doing.

After what seemed like an endless trip into the vacuum of space, Alex arrived back and realised that he had spent a long time in the woods, it was almost 5 p.m. He knew he had to be quick and warn everyone, but what was he going to say? Would they even believe him? They might think he is crazy. So many questions were going through his brain. Either way, he must get this news to the police at least to get ready for the worst. Whatever she was doing, he seemed to get the feeling that she was going to do something big. He rushed to his car, which was still there, then got in and hit the road to the police headquarters. He needed answers, whatever happens. He's always needed answers. What would stop his sister, there was absolutely nothing that could stop a ghost in Amorbis, not even the greatest scientists have had the chance to as they have never had anything to test it on after building an invention. Anne's feelings seemed pretty hurt and she was quite upset, still, about what had happened on that faithful day.

As he was going along the road to the police station, the pavements were empty, stores were shut, no cars on the road. It seemed all too quiet, not a sound was heard, and Alex wondered what had happened while he was gone. He put the radio on, and set it to the local radio station, the broadcasters were still going on about gossip that no one cared about, but then, suddenly, it all stopped. They both paused for a minute. Alex waited, tension building up, what happened? Suddenly, they both came on air again.

"Umm…we have an emergency announcement to make. Please stay at home at all times. Food will be brought around every week by special forces, who are armed, trained and protected. We have been told that the ghost of Anne Carter and the other female ghosts, which have been recognised, are now terrorising the city as well," the female presenter said anxiously, but clearly. Oh no! Alex thought. This meant his sister had already started her invasion. He was too late! But his mindset changed immediately. Was Juliet okay, she said she was going to the shopping centre with her friend and had left after he'd left to go to the police station that morning. Was she okay? What if something happened to her? But he knew he couldn't change his mind now. He was already at the police station, so it was best he went and saw what was going on. When he got to the door, they were locked. He stood, unaware of what could be lurking amongst him, on the streets, in the alley ways. He was warned but he had to get in, unfortunately, no one saw him. He kept banging on the door, hoping a human soul would enter the reception room and let him from the outdoors. After a few minutes, he'd lost any hope of a policeman or woman entering and letting him into the station. Still no reply, with all hope lost he went back to his car. Suddenly, with great surprise a policeman came to the door, opened it and looked out. It was the new Officer that he'd met today. Before he gave him a thought to close the doors that he had been pounding on frantically to get in, he stepped out and bellowed for him to not shut the door and let him in.

"Be quiet, son, the ghosts might hear you!" He whispered. For some reason, it looked as if the man was waiting for Alex to look at him, as if he were a maniac or wanted Alex to look surprised. "You're not confused as to why I said ghosts were in our town,?" he asked in bewilderment.

"No, in fact, I was coming here to warn you about this, but my sister beat me to it," He said in a hurry, "What's the situation?" he asked desperately.

"Very bad. You were very lucky son, you weren't killed. Anybody that the ghosts come across; they kill!" He said plainly, hinting that he was lucky. He knew that he was lucky now, but there was something his sister was after. There must be another factor to this. Alex already knew that she wanted revenge but then he realised something… His sister wanted revenge, and she wanted to get Harry which means she was going to come to the police station and had come for Harry. But why wasn't she here yet? he wondered, so he went to look. He peered through the glass door, cautious not to step outside. What he saw coming made him tremble. His sister was coming heavily armed with guns. She was prepared and meant business. The new police Officer forgot to mention his name the entire time that they were speaking, but for some odd reason, now he remembered to say it. It was 'Jimmy' and Alex told Jimmy to find all the policemen and tell them to get armed and protected. His sister was hovering above ground, slowly coming closer and closer. Fortunately, it wasn't a giant army of ghosts coming but they were quite a few armed and following Anne. A couple of minutes later, a whole unit of policemen and women arrived to help, holding bullet-proof barriers, guns. Jimmy said everyone was wearing bullet-proof tops and handed him one. Before the unit arrived, he thought about what he himself would do. He wasn't a highly trained professional who knew what he was doing. He was good and quickly learned things by watching and practicing, but due to the rarity of police action, he never really saw any. But now he knew what he had to do and without any consent or warning from the police, he took the gun Jimmy gave to him, an MI6A4 assault rifle, and confidently opened the door to confront his sister for doing these treacherous actions to innocent people. He went outside and didn't show any signs of weakness to his sister.

"Alex! What are you doing here? Don't get in the way of my plan," she spoke.

"I will, if this is what you plan on doing to innocent people who have done nothing to you," he bellowed at her.

"True, true. You know what, I'll spare you, you were my brother anyways," she said as if he was a pathetic sack of potatoes.

"What's happened to you? You're not the kind and loving sister I knew," He said a bit more calmly, trying to get her to remember her previous self. But it backfired.

"What happened to me!" she said, looking offended, "you are really asking me that question. You know what happened. You know what hit me harder than anything. The fact that Harry was cheating on me! But there's also something else… I never told you, but this also hurt me. Every night, I would hope that mother would come home, maybe she had heard that father was taken to rehab and that she would be back. That she actually cared about us. That she still loved us. That she was still OUR mother!" she said furiously, with tears forming in the corner of her pale, ghostly eyes. "But NO! Never! She was never there when I needed her, when I needed advice. Now get out of my way so that I can do what I came here for. Or you'll end up like them too!" she said, urging him to get out of the way just so he wouldn't get hurt. She wanted to spare him, and he could sense it, but she was still going to kill innocent people along with Harry and guilty prisoners.

"Wait!" he said demandingly "You don't think I was hurt by this? All you're thinking about is yourself. Ever since mother left and father was taken away, I had one person too look up to…and that was you. All through my life…you… you were my mother. I was five when mother left, but you've looked out for me since," he said, but he could see it did not change his sister's mood. He was pushing the limit down to the wire. He knew he was threading on thin ice. Then, without warning, she sent a missile spiralling towards the station. He looked at it, and desperate instincts kicked in, there was no way to save them. He ran as fast as he could before the explosion and due to the force of energy released, it sent him flying off his feet. Fortunately, he didn't land on his head, but was quite hurt. He managed to get himself up, but what lied ahead left him speechless, his dry mouth open, taking in the devastation that remained. Dead bodies, still leaking blood, pools of it staining the tarmac. Fire, burning the remains to crisp. It was hell right in front of him. Innocent policemen and women lay there, their lives snatched away from him only because his sister was devastated and thirsty for revenge. She had it now, and there was nothing he could do about it. But his mind turned onto his mother. What if she was still out there, maybe she could convince Anne to stop this, and after over 20 years he could meet his mother. But the key thing he needed for this plan was his mother, and she wasn't here. He then remembered Juliet; she must be worried sick about him. She may even think he's dead. What if she is! He was panicking now and wanted to get to her as quickly as he could, but his car was in pieces. It would take him about half an hour if he walked. But he saw a bike and swiftly got on it and pedalled as fast as he could back to his house. After 20 minutes of desperate pedalling and wanting to be with his wife, he arrived and instantly getting off, ran to the door. He frantically searched for the house keys and once he found them, he opened the door. It was a disaster; everything was on the floor and the house was in a mess, it was definitely rummaged. He was worried sick now and wondered where his wife could be. He went all around the house searching for her, maybe she was underneath all their belongings. Once he got to their room, he looked in his cupboard and saw a letter. It said...

Family reunion

Dear Alex,

I have gone to a safe place; it is in the woods. I have your mother, she said she has come back and has been here for around three weeks but didn't know what to do ever since your sister died. I brought her here after I saw her when I was coming back home. She looks very much the same, but is still in pain, please come to the den we built, after university. Everything will be explained once you come.

Love Juliet

xxxxxx

He was relieved and, fortunately, could still remember where the den was. With nothing else he could possibly want than being with his mother and wife, he bolted off. He was not showing it on the outside but on the inside, he was extremely happy that his mother had come back. But why so late? Why now? He asked himself. The den wasn't far and in a few minutes he was there. The one thing he wanted to see was there. It was Juliet and his mother! But she was badly injured. He gave Juliet a hug and quickly tended to his mother who was over the moon to see her son after such a long time.

Soon they started a long conversion where Alex went all out and asked many questions.

"Are you okay now, mother!" he asked.

"Yes, son, thank you so much, and thank you Juliet. You have married such a wonderful young lady; I just wish that I was there," she said, crying, as she felt guilty for leaving him at such a young age and for such a long time.

"Why didn't you come back, after you left? I always relied on Anne to take good care of me, but do you know who was hurt the most. It was Anne, she said you were never there when she needed you, I may have had her as a motherly figure, but she had no one." This made her even more guilty.

"I know but I wasn't sure what'd happened to your father, and I didn't want to face more abuse, and I didn't want you to witness it either. But here we are now, all because of me," She said, tears welling up in the corner of her eyes, her heart flooding with guilt.

"Don't say that Mum. I understand why Anne is doing this, but she shouldn't be. She should be able to forgive the past. What is she going to achieve after killing all these people, huh?" he explained, trying to reassure his mother that it wasn't her fault.

"I know Alex, but these people have suffered so much because of my cowardly decisions. Your sister is taking her anger out on other innocent people when it should be me, she's angry because I was never there to help her, especially when that cruel and selfish man cheated on her. I hear he is dead now, well actually, I guessed that, but I did hear that the police station blew up and many died," his mother explained, still ashamed of herself.

44

"Yeah, Anne came over, furious! She wanted to obliterate Harry. But Mum, how do you know that Anne will stop after she sees you?" He asked wondering what his mother might be planning. She gave a quick sigh, signalling to Alex that it may not be what he wants to hear, but she went on anyway.

"I don't know what'll happen, but I've got to stop your sister from making these people suffer more and more just because I am too scared to show my face!" she said confidently. Alex knew his mother had to do what she had to do, he couldn't be selfish; his mother was right and he knew it. But that uneasy feeling urged him to stop her from showing herself and the factor of not knowing what will happen made it even more urging to stop her. But the thought of saving all of these people and letting them be free of the terror occurring at the present moment overpowered the one of losing his mother. They went back into the main area in town, and he caught a glimpse of his sister. He shouted. An immediate reaction was shown, and at once she turned around, he could see her throw a nasty scowl at him, but then, suddenly, it changed into a face of shock. She raced down, swiftly wanting to get to her mother after such a long time.

"Mother, is that really you?" She said with astonishment.

"Yes, Anne, it is really me, but is it really you?" She said, wanting to say it furiously but seeing her daughter in such a long time made her unable to process that emotion.

"Yes, mother, it's me!" She said hurriedly, not to upset her mother, but tears started forming.

"Why were you never there for me" Anne said, but she was cut off.

"I know sweetie, Alex told me everything. I feel terrible for leaving you, but you can't take the anger you have for me on all these innocent people, please stop," she said in a soft, motherly voice, trying to get her to stop.

"Well…maybe if you come with me, we can live happily for eternity," she said, as if she had planned for this to happen all along. Of course, she didn't know but to Alex this was bomb blasting in his ears. He couldn't lose his mother again!

"NO!" He roared, making himself feel heard.

"Well then, I guess these people will live their lives happily like this, don't you think!" she said, mockingly.

"NO!" This time it was their mother, "Let me talk to Alex first, Anne," so Anne went up higher so she couldn't hear, "Alex, my dear boy, when I first left you, every night you and your sister popped up in my head and you, being only five, I wondered how you would cope, and who'd be there for you. But now I know that if you could do that, then you can do this. Think of all the people this could harm, if I'd stay here," she explained. Alex let out a low sigh and agreed reluctantly. But one thing concerned him… How was she going to take their mother with her? She was a ghost.

"Okay Anne, I'll come with you, but you must stop killing and endangering all these people," She said reluctantly. Immediately Anne blew a whistle and all her ghost army came back.

"Now, mother, you must say, 'Anne Carter may take me to the spiritual realms'" Anne said, which Alex thought seemed like it came out of a fairy tale.

"Anne Carter may take me to the spiritual realms" she said, and then Alex could see her body deteriorating until nothing was left. Silence. All Alex could hear were the blazing fires, people screaming and footsteps pounding the Earth. Then out of nowhere, his mother appeared…but in ghost form. This was what Anne wanted to do, this was how she was to take his mother. After a minute of his mother getting used to being a spectre, they said their goodbyes, and soon, abruptly left. He turned around and to his amazement, everything was forming back to normal, the fires were going away, collapsed buildings were reforming, and everything was coming into order. But a bigger surprise was awaiting him. Emerging from the reforming buildings, a familiar face came to view. It was his father, with a smile on his face and he seemed to be under control of himself. He sprinted towards him and gave him a big, long hug. He knew he wasn't alone and he knew he could cope; it was for the better.